# Searching For Love
## —— In All The ——
# Wrong Places

*Also by Ina Perkins . . .*

Hey Teacher . . . Real Talk!
Hey Parent . . . Real Talk!

# SEARCHING FOR LOVE
## —— IN ALL THE ——
# WRONG PLACES

*Poems by DeOndre Chambers*

## INA PERKINS

iUniverse LLC
Bloomington

**Searching For Love In All The Wrong Places**

iUniverse books may be ordered through booksellers or by contacting:

iUniverse LLC
1663 Liberty Drive
Bloomington, IN 47403
www.iuniverse.com
1-800-Authors (1-800-288-4677)

ISBN: 978-1-4917-1880-3 (sc)
ISBN: 978-1-4917-1881-0 (e)

Library of Congress Control Number: 2013923000

Printed in the United States of America.

iUniverse rev. date: 01/07/2014

# ACKNOWLEDGMENTS

Given honor and praise to the King of kings and the Lord of lords, Jesus Christ the Savior of my soul.

**I thank God** for blessing me with a multitude of people that have played a major part in my life knowingly and unknowingly.

**I thank God** for my mother Betty Chambers a strong and unmovable mother that has never allowed the issues of life to stop her. As I grow in age I see her strength and determination in me more and more.

**I thank God** for my sisters Sharman and Vanessa who was there supporting and encouraging me when I was a young teen-age single mother searching for love and trying to raise my children.

**I thank God** for my children DeOndre and LaBetra who has always loved me even when I felt unlovable and didn't deserve their love because of decisions and mistakes I made along the way as a young single mother.

**I thank God** for my stepchildren Maryann and Edie who has also played a hand in the molding and shaping of the woman that I am today.

**I thank God** for Rev. Michael Coleman and First Lady Coleman for their wisdom and love for me as I struggled through times in my life.

**I thank God** for Stella Thomas and Rosemary Jordan for being friends that would edify and encourage at all times.

**I thank God** for Charletta Sudduth who helped me to stay the course. For William Bradford for his unselfish love.

**I thank God** for Bishop Taylor and First Lady Taylor for teaching me how to speak life and walk in it.

**I thank God** for Minister Antonio Davis for believing in me and speaking life to me.

**I thank God** for David and Sandy Faust for helping me to move to another level spiritually by the love that they have shown me and the words of life they have spoken to me.

**A special thanks to God** for my Priest, Prophet, King, Ruler and over comer, my husband Mr. Eddie A. Perkins. A soldier of the Lords' who have been knocked down many of times along life's' journey but is still standing! Standing stronger than ever before! Standing for righteousness, a mighty warrior for the Lord. Continue to stand strong because when you stand strong, I stand strong!

# AUTHOR'S NOTE

Searching for Love, a Christian fiction book, was birth forth through the realities of life (children, self, people, and issues). It is written in letter format going against what is considered a normal manuscript, but what does it mean to be normal anyway?

Going with the majority?

Allowing people, circumstances, and life to determine who you are and put limits on who you are.

Why can't normalcy mean stepping out of the boat and walking on water. Taking the limits off of yourself and being all that God says that you are! Included in the back section of this book are poems written from the mind of my dear son, Deondre. Written from his life experiences as he searched for purpose and meaning in life. Some poems were written from different stages and seasons of his life. Some poems were written from different geographical locations, from the comfort of his bedroom to the harshness of a prison cell.

# Introduction

Have you ever been one out searching for real love?

You know a love that loves at all times?

A love that no matter how much you weigh it will always stay.

A love that loves no matter how short your hair, it's always there.

A love that loves no matter what color your skin, it still lets you in.

A love that loves no matter what you have done wrong, it still grows strong.

A love that loves you when you are unlovable. It never lets you go.

A love that loves you when you're messed up from the floor up, physically, mentally, emotionally, and spiritually!

A love that gives you hope when you have no hope!

A love that bears all and never falls.

An unconditional love.

In her search for love, Yours Truly, finally finds and experiences the perfect love but not before the issues of life impacts her spiritually, physically, emotionally, and mentally. In Squirrel's journey for love, life's challenges and generational curses forces him into the arms of an unconditional love that changes his life forever!

# Squirrel speaks:
# Life in the Eyes of Squirrel

**Hey Yours Truly:**

All I want is your booty I don't need your mind, your intellect, your inner being, nor your beauty. I don't need to know your likes and dislike, your dreams or passions. I don't need to know about your family and you don't need to know about mines. See, all I want is your booty and anything else you can give me to make my life better like money, clothes, cologne, and jewelry.

See, I can't make a commitment to you only, can't leave my other ladies lonely. I can't mess up my good thing just for you. See right now I just need to get down with getting my needs met and when I feel you can't do that anymore, I'll just move to the booty next door. I know I left you hanging with AIDS, babies, low self-esteem and insecurities. You see this is my world and I'm just a squirrel trying to get a nut. I can't mess up my world trying to please you boo. I can't make a commitment to only you. I can't help take care of babies that my sperm helped to make, see there is just too many of them. Oh. I forgot to tell you. I already have five babies by five different ladies and yours make six.

See, I'm just a squirrel living in this world trying to get a nut. It's easier to be a squirrel in this world than to stand up and be a man. A man what is that? I never had a real man in my life a man that would stand up to his responsibilities. I only had squirrels in my life, males running away from their responsibilities. So I choose to stay a squirrel than to become a man because right now it seems to be meeting my every need! I don't know maybe one day I will turn all this over and seek to become a man, a real man.

**P.S.** I forgot to tell you that I am also a drug dealer. I must sell drugs because I got so many baby mommas that if I dare to work child support would truly hurt. So I choose to make my money the illegal way because I truly don't believe that I will have to pay or I don't care about the consequences at least not today!

**Squirrel**

# Yours Truly speaks:
## But Squirrel

**Squirrel:**

You are not the first and probably won't be the last person that just wants me for my body. Believe it or not Squirrel, I have been going through this long before you. I watched my mom go through this also I'm sure she watched her mom go through it to. You may not love me now but I know soon you'll love me the way that I love you. I see you with your other ladies but I'm not tripping as long as I get my time with you. As far as a commitment, I'm not expecting that from you right now. I know that you have a lot of needs and need more than one woman to supply them. It's cool if you got five babies by five different ladies, because I have three babies by three different maybes and yours make four. I named them all after their daddies/maybes. There is John III, Roy II, Troy Jr. and now Squirrel VI. Even though you didn't know my children's names nor don't claim the baby your sperm helped make, I still know that you love me because you always tell me so. I love you too, can't you tell, because my children go without so I can meet your needs without a doubt. See, I don't have much but what I have is yours first and fore most. I don't have a high school diploma or GED (General Education Diploma) but that's ok because I got ADC (Aid to Dependent Children). They tell me that in the next two years I will be cut off of ADC but I can't worry about two years from now I can only see what's in front of me now.

Squirrel, I know you can't help me take care of my children but somehow they will survive. You see I survived; my father was named Squirrel too. He rejected me like so many other squirrels, but the hurt of the rejection of a parent cannot be compared to anything else. It's a hurt that never goes away. A hurt that tries to raise its ugly head in every area of life. A hurt that tries to keep you from trusting others. A hurt that hurts at all times. My father was a squirrel, he always ran away from his responsibilities, never worked because he said child support would truly hurt. He tried selling drugs until he fell in love with the drugs and now he's doing time for trying to rob to buy a dime. Squirrel you remind me so much of my dad, I wonder if that's why I love you so, looking to you to give me that love that I never received from my dad. See, my dad was never around to show me what love looks like or feels like in a relationship. See, my dad was never there to tell me that I have pretty hair. See, my dad was never there to teach me how to care. He was never there to tell me that I was somebody created to achieve great things. My dad was never there! Squirrel don't you see why I need your love so very bad that I don't care what disease you may have.

**Yours Truly**

# Yours Truly speaks: Life's Questions (the life changing question)

**Squirrel:**

I have been looking back over my life and asking myself some really deep questions about life like . . .

What is life?

Is there purpose and meaning in my life?

What have I accomplished so far in my life?

Am I living a life to be proud of?

What kind of impact am I making on my children's life and others?

Am I a mother that my children can be proud of?

If I was to die today what would people say about the life I lived?

I also asked myself the questions that really helped me to want a changed life. I asked myself what would my children grow up to be? . . . Would they be like me? In asking myself these questions I came to realize that I was living a life that I didn't want my children to repeat. I don't want my children to be like me so I must start now letting them know that they are somebody created to achieve great things. Squirrel, because of a mother's love for her children I must let you go. See I have been searching for love in all the wrong places now I must look in the right place. Lord please help me!

**Yours Truly**

# GOD SPEAKS:
## OH DON'T YOU KNOW
## THAT I LOVE YOU SO

**Yours Truly:**

I just want you to know that I love you so. It started way back in time even before you were born. Yours Truly, I am your Creator. You were in my care even before you were born (Isaiah 44: 2a). Yours Truly, I know everything about you. I know every strand of hair on your head (Matthew 10:30); I know every bone in your body. See I fearfully and wonderfully made you just for me (Psalm. 139:14). See you are not a mistake. You may have been conceived in sin but sin did not win. I created you and placed you on this earth for my purpose. See, I am God and I never make mistakes. Yours Truly, when you were born, you were born in sin because of the sin of one man, whose name is Adam. Because of this man's sin, you must be born again (Spiritual Rebirth). Let me explain what sin is. Sin is anything people do or say that doesn't please me, which goes against my word, the Bible.

Because of the nature of your flesh (your body) which is to want to sin, I had to send my Only Begotten Son Jesus to earth to shed His blood and to redeem (buy back) man from the death of sin.

For the wages of sin is death; but the gift of God is external life through Jesus Christ (Romans 6:23).

Yours Truly, I love you so because I Am Love. Whether or not you feel loved, regardless of what you have done or where you have come from, I love you. See my love for you is unconditional. There is nothing you can say or do to make me not love you. There is nothing that can separate you from my love (Romans 8:38-39). Yes, Yours Truly, you have been searching for love in all the wrong places but I see in your heart that you sincerely want to experience the love that I have for you.

**P.S.** I am so glad that you asked yourself the life changing questions, what will my children grow up to be? Will they be like me? What a very wise question for a mother to ask herself.

**God**

**Hey God:**

It's Yours Truly!

God how in the world can a person be born again? Surely a person cannot enter a second time into his mother's womb to be born (John 3:4)! It just doesn't make any sense to me! How can this be?

# GOD SPEAKS:
## UNCONDITIONAL LOVE

**Yours Truly:**

Well, Yours Truly, you were first born of your mothers' womb but in order to enter into the Kingdom of Heaven you must be born again spiritually which is called Salvation. Flesh gives birth to flesh, but the Spirit gives birth to spirit (John 3:6). Salvation means to accept Christ as your Lord and Savior and commit your life to Him, to receive my spirit and to have a right relationship with me (John3: 3-5). See, Yours Truly, salvation is a gift from me. There is nothing that is within your power that can assist you in receiving this gift (Ephesians 2:8). Yours Truly, all humans have sinned, and come short of my glory (Romans 3:23) even the squirrels that are in your life or have been in your life. Yours Truly, I love you but I also love all the squirrels that have played a part in your life. My desire is that no one should parish but live with me in Heaven forever (John 3:16). I am a God of love (1John 4:8b). I don't hate the sinner, I hate the sin. I am also a just God and because I hate sin I must punish sin. I had to send my Only Beloved Son Jesus Christ to earth to die on the cross to pay the penalty for your sins and He rose from the grave to purchase a place for you in Heaven. Yours

Truly, you must believe and trust that Jesus died and rose again for you so you can have eternal life. Yours Truly, you must also be willing to turn from anything that is not pleasing to me, this is called repentance.

So to clarify what you need to do to receive Salvation (to be born again spiritually) you must transfer your trust and belief from what you have been doing to what Christ has done for you on the cross. You must accept Christ as your Savior, open the door to your heart and ask Him to come in (Revelations 3:20). You must receive Jesus Christ as Lord. Give Him the controls of every area of your life, and you must repent. This is what Being Born Again Spiritually is all about.

God

# Yours Truly speaks:
# But God I Am So Unworthy Of Your Love

**God:**

Wow, God, you seem to be asking a lot from a person when asking them to be born again! And what about all my short comings because I am far from perfect and I don't see how I can every live a perfect life! God, I have all these babies by all these different squirrels and a couple of them I am not sure who their daddy is. I dislike myself, I have AIDS, and I am just so unworthy of your love and your gift of Salvation. I don't know your word but I know I must be one of the biggest sinners if not the chief sinner!

**Yours Truly**

# GOD SPEAKS:
# LOVE COVERS A
# MULTITUDE OF SINS

**Yours Truly:**

Yours Truly, what I am asking you to do to be born again is truly nothing compared to what my Son Jesus has done for you. See, you could never repay Jesus for all that He has done for you, never!

Yes, Yours Truly, you are so unworthy of my love and my gift of Salvation. That is why I had to send my Son Jesus to earth to take all that unworthiness and your entire past, present and future sins to the cross with Him. See, Jesus has overcome sin; He has taken the power out of sin. So because of what Jesus did you can overcome sin through Jesus. Sin will not have power over your life any more. If you have a bible I want you to read Romans chapter eight verses one through seventeen to learn more on being freed from sin. Yours Truly, I am a forgiving God. If you bring your sins before me and ask for forgiveness with a sincere heart I will forgive you. By accepting Jesus Christ as your Lord and Savior, my spirit, the Holy Spirit, will live in you to help you to live. My spirit will communicate my truth to you, convict you of sin, convince you that my ways are right, comfort you when you are sad and guide you. My spirit the Holy Spirit will give you gifts and godly characteristics called the Fruit of the Spirit (Gal. 5:22-23).

So, Yours Truly, if you are ready to give me the control of your life you can pray the following prayer of repentance:

Dear Lord,

I come asking that you please forgive me for all the wrong things that I have done in my life. I believe that your Son Jesus died on the Cross-for my sins and that He rose on the third day. I thank you that he is now in Heaven interceding on my behalf. Lord I come asking that you come into my life and be the Lord of my life. I am ready to turn my will and trust over to you, have your way in every area of my life for the rest of my life. In Jesus name I pray Amen.

**God**

# Yours Truly speaks:
# Peace That Passeth
# All Understanding

**God**

I thank you for your highest blessing, your peace! Ever since I prayed the prayer of repentance my spirit has been at peace. It has been a peace that passeth all understanding (Philippians 4:7). I truly can't understand it because I am still battling with the same battles in my life! I am still a single parent on ADC trying to make ends meet, who is dying from AIDS. But since I prayed the prayer of repentance a change has come over me. I feel like I can handle whatever may come my way. Lord I thank you for perfect peace because I now keep my mind on you and my trust is in you (Isaiah 26: 3). Thank you Lord for showing yourself real in my life and for being a faithful God. I thank you for being a God that will never leave me nor forsake me (Heb.13: 5).

**Yours Truly**

# Squirrel speaks:
## Hey Yours Truly:

It's Squirrel, what's up! I need some money. Can you give me about fifty dollars? I will pay you back. And where have you been? I haven't heard from you in a long time. Do you have a new man or what? Oh, I forgot you asked yourself that life changing question. So does that mean your life changed? And now you think that you and your children are better than everyone else. Any way let me know if you can give me some money!

**Later, Squirrel**

# Esther speaks:
## New Life

**Squirrel:**

Do you really want to know what's up? Well let me tell you regardless if you really want to know or not! First of all Squirrel, my days of taking care of you are over, so please don't ever again ask me for money! And yes, I do have a new man and his name is Jesus! My relationship with him has given me a new life. See, because of what he has done for me, I am free. I am free from the power of sin (Romans 8:2). I have found real love. A love that will heal me from all past, present and future hurts and pain. A love that has forgiven me for all my wrong doings. It's because of this love that I don't have to sleep around to feel loved. I don't have to continue to conceive babies in sin. You know now it's ok that my daddy was a squirrel, that he never told me how pretty I am or that I was a somebody created to do great things. I know now that regardless of what my past was it's only through my relationship with Christ Jesus that I now know that I was created to do great things. See, He knows all about me because He fearfully and wonderfully made me when I was in my mother's womb (Palms 139:13-14). He is also forgiving. He has forgiven me for all the wrong things that I have ever done in my life and He wants the best for my children and me.

Oh yea Squirrel because of this relationship I have changed my name and the names of my children. My new name is now Esther; Esther was the Queen of Persia in the Bible. She was a woman of great courage; she saved her Jewish people from destruction. God has given me great courage to turn from the sinful life that I once lived, to a new life of serving Him. I also changed my children's names to Joshua, Caleb, Isaiah and Israel. See in the Bible Joshua and Caleb had courage to stand up against the majority in believing that the Israelites could conquer the Canaanites (Numbers 14:6-9). As my sons Joshua and Caleb become young men they will have the courage to stand up for what's right and pleasing to God and standup to their responsibilities of being real men and not to become squirrels. They must help to pass this courage and knowledge down to their younger brothers whose names have been changed to Isaiah and Israel. In the Bible Isaiah emphasizes the importance of righteousness and justice toward others and Israel means ruling with God.

Squirrel, I have learned that as parents, the choices that we make in our lives will affect our children (Deuteronomy 30:19). As parents we can speak blessings or curses upon our children's lives (Proverbs 18:21). So the change must start with me, because I want to live a life that is going to bless my children not curse them. Squirrel because of this wonderful change in my life I am a new person. My old way of living is no more (2 Corinthians 5:17). Squirrel, I don't think that my children and I are better than everyone else because the new life that I now live you can live it to. Salvation is a free gift from God; all you have to do is invite Jesus into your heart. Squirrel I will be praying for you.

**Esther**

# Squirrel speaks:
# Don't Change My Name!

**Hey Yours Truly I mean Esther:**

Are you ok because you have been talking all this crazy stuff talking about a new life, changing your name and your children's names, and me inviting Jesus into my heart. You must be on some kind of drugs or something. And If inviting Jesus into my life mean that I would have to become a real man and stand up to my responsibilities of taking care of all my children, work a real job, and give up chasing booty, than I choose to stay a squirrel. I just can't see life being better than the life that I now live. I can have all the ladies I want and they take care of me and meet my every need! I just can't see letting all that go! Oh yeah, Esther I was just playing, I don't need your money or nothing else from you.

**PS.** Please don't pray for me. Pray for yourself. It sounds like you need it, not me.

**Later,**
**Squirrel**

# Esther speaks:
# God I Must Let Them Know

**God:**

Why won't Squirrel accept your free gift of Salvation? God can't you make him change? Oh God, so many of my friends is living the life that I used to live. They are having babies after babies by so many different squirrels. Some of them are not sure who their babies' daddies are. God, I just don't want to sit around and not share my new life with them. I want to let them know that life doesn't have to be empty, meaningless and without purpose. I want to let them know that the life you have for them is a life of good and not of evil to give them a future and a hope. (Jeremiah 29: 11).

**Esther**

# God Speaks:
## You Are My Disciple

**My Daughter Esther:**

I feel your sincere desire for the Salvation of Squirrel. At this time in Squirrel's life he thinks that everything is going well. He gets pleasure out of the life that he now lives and can't see the need to change or except the gift of Salvation. He thinks his way is the right way but there is a way that seems right to a man, but the end thereof are ways of destruction (Proverbs 16:25). I Am God and I can make him change but I am not a God that forces himself on others. I want Squirrel to see his need for me because it's not until he sees the need that he will live for me. Esther you must continue to pray for him. Pray that he will receive my free gift before it is ever too late and continue to witness to him as my Spirit leads you.

Esther, you are called to be my disciple (follower of Jesus) and yes you must tell of the Good News of Jesus Christ. Tell it everywhere you go so that a lost world can be freed from the power of sin!

Yes, you must let your family, friends and even your enemies know.

You must let them know that I love them so.

You must let them know that they are searching for love in all the wrong places that it's not in the bars, gangs, squirrels, sex, clothes, cars, drugs, money, pride or material things.

You must let them know that the life they now live will come to an end one day and when this life is over ask them where they will spend eternity.

You must let them know that babies don't give love they take love.

You must let them know that when they have sex outside of marriage they are committing a sin called fornication.

You must let them know that your God hates sin and that there are consequences for sin (Romans 6:23).

You must let them know that their body is a living temple for the Lord and the use of drugs, alcohol, fornication, and all that is against God's will is killing this temple (1Corinthians 3: 16).

You must let them know that living a life without Christ is living a life of hopelessness and an empty life a life with no purpose!

Please let them know that I love them so!

**God**

# Squirrel speaks:
## Knocking On Death's Door

**Hey Yours Truly I mean Esther:**

It's me Squirrel. I am in the intensive care unit of Mount Mercy Hospital. Esther I am so sick! The doctors say that I am in the last stages of the AIDS disease and no one has been here to see me, no body! Not my mother, not by brothers, not my ladies or any of my children! Esther I never would have thought that my family, friends and children would let me down like this! They all know that I need them now. Esther, I just don't understand this life, what have I done to deserve this? I'll tell you, nothing! I have done nothing to deserve this physical pain that I am in, nothing to deserve this AIDS Disease that has taken over my body, I don't have any energy, frequent fevers and sweats, large lymph nodes, skin rashes, painful sores on my mouth and genitals areas. I've got a painful nerve disease called Shingles. I have coughing, shortness of breath, painful swallowing, severe and persistent diarrhea; vomiting, abdominal cramps, severe headaches and I have loss so much weight! I don't deserve this! I don't deserve to be treated like this by the people that say they love me! No one loves me, no one! Maybe I should just go ahead and die. No one would even care.

**Squirrel**

# Esther Speaks:
## Reap What You Sow

**Squirrel:**

Where in the world do you get off thinking that you are so perfect! Well, let me help you out by letting you know firsthand! Yes, you do deserve everything that you are getting right now and then some! Squirrel you have hurt so many people and especially me! Don't you remember that I have a son by you that you have never claimed nor done anything for! You are always taking from others but never giving to others! You think that the world owes you everything but it doesn't! You have given me AIDS and ain't no telling who else! See, Squirrel I am the wrong one to be singing your sad song to. You need to save that for the Oprah show maybe they will have sympathy for you because right now I have none! It's because of your selfish ways that my children might have to grow up without a mother!

**Esther**

# ESTHER SPEAKS:
# LORD HELP!

**God:**

I come to you with much anger and hurt in my heart! God I know that your word says it is ok to be angry but don't let your anger cause you to sin (Ephesians 4:26). God you are going to have to help me with this one because right about now anything is possible! See, I heard from Squirrel today and he tried to make it seem like he is so perfect and that he has never done anyone wrong! But he has wronged many people and that is why he is in the hospital right now very sick! He wants someone to show him some sympathy but see God I ain't the one. No, I ain't the one! After all the hurt, pain, and suffering that he has caused my children and me! I don't care what happens to him! I don't care if he dies and goes to hell! I just don't care!

**Esther**

# GOD SPEAKS:
# I AM YOUR BURDEN BEARER

**My Child Esther:**

I am so glad that you brought your anger, hurt and pain to me in prayer. I want you to lay your burdens on me, because I care for you and my yoke is easy and by burdens are light (Matthew 11:28-30). Which means that I want you to bring all your cares, worries, hurts and pains to me in prayer with the belief that I am working things out in your life because I know the thoughts that I think towards you, thoughts of peace, and not of evil, to give you a future and a hope (Jeremiah 29:11).

Esther, when you made the decision to give me the controls of your life, you also made the decision to forgive others. See, Esther, because of what Jesus did on the Cross you can freely come to me and ask for forgiveness. In my word it says; and forgive us our debts, as we forgive our debtors (Matthew 6:12) and for if ye forgive men their trespasses, I will also forgive you (Matthew 6:14). This means that if you want me to forgive you for your sins you must first forgive those that have hurt you. I know sometimes this can be hard but my spirit, the Holy Spirit, is on the inside of you to help you with this process. So don't hesitate try me and see that I am faithful to my word!

**God**

# ESTHER SPEAKS:
# THE POWER OF FORGIVENESS

**Squirrel:**

The last time that you heard from me I had said some really mean things to you. I want to apologize for the mean words that I said to you. Squirrel I was so mad at you but I prayed about it and God is taking me through the healing process so writing this letter is part of that healing process. I am now able to forgive you for **all** the hurt and pain you have caused me but I couldn't have done it without the Lord. You know Squirrel just like I forgave you; God wants to forgive you also for all of your sins if you would just ask Him with a sincere heart. You know what else, God is a healer. He is able to not just heal your spirit but also your physical body if you would just give Him the controls of your life. God is ready to start healing you from the inside out, from past, present, and future hurts if you would just let Him. Squirrel I am truly praying that you would accept God's free gift of salvation so that He can start the healing process in your life.

**Esther**

# Squirrel speaks:
# Are You Real God or
# Just An Illusion

**Hey God:**

This is Squirrel. You know God Esther is always talking about this God that has changed her life. She has even changed her name and her children's names. God if you are as real as Esther says you are and if you are a God of love and a God that works miracles why have you allowed me to live the life that I have been living? Why have you allowed me to get the AIDS Disease? Why are you allowing me to lie on my deathbed? The doctors tell me that I can die at any time. I am knocking on death's door and not only that but you are allowing me to die ALONE! No one has been up here to see me NO ONE! You know God I really wonder just how real you are! God if you are so real:

Where were you when my mother was too young to know how to be a real mother?

Where were you God when my daddy didn't want to have anything to do with me?

Where were you God when I was pretty much raising my siblings and myself?

Where were you God when my peers in school were teasing me?

Where were you God when I got beat up by a gang of guys that I thought were my friends?

Where were you God when I was so confused about life and how I fit in this thing called life?

Where were you God when my hormones were going crazy and I had no one to talk to about the way I was feeling and why didn't you stop me from acting out on those feelings?

Where were you God when this AIDS virus came upon my body?

God why when the times I needed you most you were not there for me?!

Where were you God?!!

**Squirrel**

# GOD SPEAKS:
# I WAS THERE!

**My Dearest Squirrel:**

I Am El ROI, the God who sees you and knows everything about you. Squirrel, I know your down sitting and uprising, I understand your thought from afar. I am acquainted with all your

ways. I know every word in your tongue. I have my hand upon you. Squirrel such knowledge is too wonderful and high for you to attain. Squirrel, if you shall go from my spirit or flee from my presence, I am there. If you ascend up into heaven, I am there. Squirrel, if you take the wings of the morning, and dwell in the uttermost parts of the sea; even there shall my hand lead you, and my right hand shall hold you. Squirrel, I made all the delicate, inner parts of your body. I knitted them together in your mother's womb. I have fearfully and wonderfully made you. Marvelous are my works. Squirrel, I saw you before you were born. I scheduled each day of your life before you began to breathe. Every day of your life was recorded in my book. Squirrel, how precious are my thoughts towards you, Oh Squirrel, how great is the sum of them! If you should count them, they are more in number than the sand. My thoughts are constantly towards you. When you awake, I am still with you

Squirrel (Psalms 139). Squirrel, I am omnipresent which means I am present everywhere. Squirrel, I have been with you before you were born and through every season of your life even to this point and time in your life. Squirrel, I have purpose and destiny for your life. I know the thoughts that I think toward you, thought of peace, and not of evil, to give you an expected end (Jeremiah 29:11).

So, the answer to your question, "Where were you God?" is . . . I was there! I was there making you, molding you, forming you, holding you, comforting you, watching you, caring for you, speaking to you, listening to you, and loving you. Squirrel, I love you so much that I sent my only begotten Son Jesus to die on the Cross just for you, for your sins (John 3:16). So you can have a personal relationship with me and so that you can live a fulfilled life the abundant life that Jesus died to give you. Squirrel, I am present everywhere. I have been with you before you were born. Squirrel, all the energy and time that you used to chase after women and material things, use it now to chase after me. Seek me Squirrel, while I can be found (Isaiah 55:6). I promise if you will dwell with me I will dwell with you. Confess my name, believe in me, repent, turn from your sinful ways and I will give you new life!

**EL ROI**
**The God that sees and knows everything**

# Squirrel speaks:
## LIVE

**Hey God:**

You are real!

As I meditated on who you are EL ROI, the God who sees me and knows everything about me, I began looking back over my life and all that I have ever gone through and I realized that you must be real because I made it through all that life has handed to me. Now that I am on the other side of some of life experiences, I know now that I am still here today only because of you God.

God, as I meditated on who you are I begin feeling your love, your peace, and your joy. God, I see life differently now. God, please forgive me for all the hurt and pain I have caused others, please forgive me for all the wrong things that I have done in my life! God, I want to live and not die! I want to experience the fulfilled and abundant life that your Son Jesus died to give me. God, I thank you so much for sending your best, your Son Jesus to die for a sinful person like me. God, I give my life to you, please take control of my life. I want to live for you. I have messed up my life and the life of so many others.

I am now ready to live!!!

**Squirrel**

# God Speaks:
# Be Ye Healed!

**My Son Squirrel:**

Oh, what a great thing you have done. You have given me the controls of your life and because of this you should live and not die! You are now a new creation in Christ, the old has gone, the new has come (2 Corinthians 5:17)! Squirrel, you must allow me to heal the hurt from your past so you can walk into your present and grab hold of your future. You must live a life that will bring glory to my name and not shame. My Holy Spirit now dwells on the inside of you to help you live for me.

**P.S.** Squirrel, I am also Jehovah-Rophe, which means God your healer. I have healed you, restored you and made you whole, spiritually, emotionally, mentally and physically. Squirrel your sins are forgiven.

Be Ye Healed!

**Jehovah-Rophe**
**God your Healer**

# TIMOTHY SPEAKS:
# A CHANGED PERSON

**Esther**

I am new! I have a new way of thinking! I have a new Spirit, the Holy Spirit (God's Spirit) dwelling on the inside of me! I am now a new person! I've been healed spiritually and physically! I've been healed from AIDS. The doctors and nurses can't believe it!

Esther, I had an encounter with God! I found out that everything that you have been telling me about God is true. God is REAL and He loves me and knows everything about me! Oh, Esther I am so excited about this new look on life that I now have!

Esther, I am now out of the hospital. I am totally healed no sign of the AIDS Virus in my body, praise Jehovah-Rophe, the God who heals! I have gone and made amends to those that I have hurt over my life and I have forgiven those that have hurt me. Only through my relationship with God was I able to forgive, I even forgave myself.

Esther, I am so sorry for all the hurt and pain that I have caused you and your children. Words can not express how sorry I am for giving you AIDS. Esther I am pleading with you to please, please forgive me for everything that I have done wrong to you and your children. I know that it won't change the past but I am truly so, so sorry! Esther, I am now ready to stand up and be a real man, I am now ready to take on my responsibilities with the help of God. Esther, I too have changed my name. See, Squirrel means males running away from their responsibilities. I am now a new person in Christ so I am no longer running from my responsibilities but I am running to them. Because of this newness of life I have changed my name to Timothy, which means honoring God. I want to honor God, serve God and live a life that will glorify His name for the rest of my life! Esther, one way I must honor God is by being that father that God has called me to be. So Esther can I please start spending time with my son to build a father/son relationship with him. Esther I want generational cures to stop right here with me! I am now in right standing with God, and because of this, my son will not have to go through some of the things that I went through in life.

Please Esther, forgive me!

**Timothy**

# Timothy speaks:
## Return to Sender

**Hey God:**

What is going on! Today I got a return to sender letter back that I had sent to Esther. In the letter I was telling her that I had turned my life over to you and pleading with her to forgive me for all the hurt and pain that I had caused her and her children. I told her that I was ready to stand up to my responsibilities as a father.

God what is going on!

Why did this letter come back?

**Timothy**

# God speaks:
## Joy Cometh Again

**My Son Timothy:**

Esther's destiny on earth has been fulfilled. She is now home with me in Heaven. The Holy City; where I have wiped away all the tears from her eyes. Where there is no more death, sorrow, crying, nor pain (Revelations 21:4).

Timothy, know that Esther has forgiven you and I have too. My son this is a time for you to mourn knowing that you will not see Esther again in this life but know that weeping endure for a short time and then joy comes again. Timothy to everything there is a season, and a time to every purpose (Ecclesiastics 3:1). As I comfort you through this time in your life know that I will also be ordering your steps into your purpose (Ps. 37:23). It's your time to step into your season and purpose. See Timothy I have put purpose on the inside of you for my pleasure and glory. So, go ahead and mourn for Esther but know this is for a short time.

**God,**
**Your Comforter**

**God:**

If I had wings I would fly away!

**Timothy**

# POEMS FROM THE MIND OF DEONDRE

Included in this section of the book are poems written from the mind of my dear son Deondre. Written from life experiences as he searched for purpose and meaning in life. Some poems were written from different seasons and stages of his life, some written from different geographical locations, from the comfort of his bedroom to the harshness of a prison cell.

# MY LOVE FOR THE PEN

My words, my hand, my love for the pen.
My writing, my reciting, where do I began?
So cold, behold, another masterpiece unfolds.
For your pleasure, it gets better, I present you my
   treasure.
Will I stop? I hope not, except when the casket
   drops.
Until then I'll win! Me and my pen.

# MY DRUM

My drum beats different, and so I march.
I'm not defined by anyone person, thing, or force
    and so I march.
I'm stuffed with all the good things 100% (BSE).
    That's best stuff ever, and so I march.
God don't make junk and I'm not a garbage can.
    I was not sent here for you to put your trash in.
I am the head and not the tail, an ever changing
    entity. That is me.
A Man before all, I've build kingdoms and
    watched them fall.
I have failed and so I win and I've been weak but
    developed tough skin.
I have become everything in one; the sun, the
    moon, rain and pain, simple and complex,
    there's not a word made that can define
    me yet.
I'm Heaven sent, and at once Hell bound. I search
    for the truth when there's lies all around.
I have opened up my mind, my heart and soul.
I sit at the table he prepared with my foes.
I let the light he gave, shine brighter than a
    man made.
I have become a strong black male, who's not
    afraid to fail and God orders my steps from
    the start.
He beats the drum and so I march.

# LESS OF A MESS

The more I sit and contemplate on
what words I want to say.
I realize that I'm a mess
My mind it moves a mile a minute.
My skin sometimes not comfortable in it.
And I'm a mess
Mistakes I seem to make at will.
My good intent, bad decisions conceal.
I'm a mess
I present myself in all my perfections.
In hopes that you don't change directions.
And there you were, right front and center.
With help and love for this here sinner.
You've stood by me on my simple quest.
My quest to become, less of a mess.

# GROWN MAN'S WISH

Momma, I got a clue now!
It's starting to make sense
I use to wish to be grown
Damn was I wrong.
Now I pray to be strong, in a life that's so long.
Wish I was a kid, and took heed to all you said.
I pray to be strong, stand firm and hold on.
Wish I never wished that I could be grown.
What would I give,
For another whopping,
A bowl full of the knowledge that you was
    cooking.
A chance to just smile, when all I did was frown.
What would I give,
To be in your arms.
A child of yours safe from all harm.
I'd crawl before I'd walk
Learn to think before I talk.
What would I give?
I'd give all of this.
Oh to be a kid again.
And to redo that wish.

# THE REAL ME

Who am I?

I'm the shit, but don't you wish that was it?

I'm me and I'm you too, the you that you'd be if
you could be me.

I'm the color of love to unique to see.

I'm a thought that passed and I've just begun.

I. Am. The. One. Loved by few, hated by many.

Why? Because on my bad day I'm better than you.

Whatever you hope to do, I can do.

Wait what's that you say? You didn't know Dre
could snap that way.

Well, welcome to my dream, your nightmare, the
moment I decided to share.

T
A
N
G
L
E
D

W
E
B

Looking at the atrocities of the city I see outside
my window.
My mind leads me to believe that oh what a
tangled web we weave.
When children enjoy happy crack and grown men
don't know how to act. My mind leads me to
believe, oh what a tangle web we weave.
When Mother's dress to impress, and kids look
like what's left. My mind leads me to believe,
oh what a tangle web we weave.
When respect can't be gave, to the person that's
about to go in their grave. My mind leads me
to believe, oh what a tangle web we weave.
The life we lead. We plant the seed. What's done
for greed we'll reap in deed.
My mind it leads and I do believe that oh what a
tangled web we weave . . .

# OH ME/OH MY

Oh me, oh my, not again.
Is falling in love a spring time trend?
Could I be in love with the swipes of a pen?
Pull one dagger out my heart, just to put one in.
Oh me, oh my, please explain.
It must be that I love the feeling of pain.
Do I close out the sun, but welcome the rain?
Seek out the bad so I can complain.
Oh me, oh my, for one time only.
Let this be real love, and nothing phony.
Can it be more than two people horny?
Maybe for once, true matrimony.
Oh me, oh my, can I let go.
Push my past aside and start healing slowly
So that finally maybe I can grow.
All bullshit aside I want to know!

# STUPID IS, AS STUPID DOES

If stupid is as stupid does, then there's no hope for
you cuz.
If dumb reflects off what you neglect, than am I
correct to assume you lack respect?
You've seemed to failed the test of life. You can't
prevail if mistakes done twice.
For forward growth, you must rehearse. Or are
you better off in a hearse?
You're wasting skin, and will not win, till you
begin to look within and heal yourself, deal
with undealt.
True confessions of sin, release yourself. Open
your mind and move forward on time, no
further rewind the past can't define.
The rain clouds will part, and sunshine will
start as soon as you search for your way out
the dark.

**Part Two of this book coming soon!**
**The Journey of a Single Father**